December 2008

Christmas greetings

and a gift from...

**The Rotary Club
of Pleasant Hill**

1953–2008

Michele Turner

Member, Rotary Club of Pleasant Hill

Steve Wallace

Steve Wallace, Club President

Christopher Counting

To Yosef, who is very good at counting.

PATRICIA LEE GAUCH, EDITOR

PHILOMEL BOOKS
A division of Penguin Young Readers Group.
Published by The Penguin Group. Penguin Group (USA) Inc.,
375 Hudson Street, New York, NY 10014, U.S.A.
Penguin Group (Canada), 90 Eglinton Avenue East, Suite 700, Toronto, Ontario M4P 2Y3, Canada
(a division of Pearson Penguin Canada Inc.). Penguin Books Ltd, 80 Strand, London WC2R 0RL,
England. Penguin Ireland, 25 St. Stephen's Green, Dublin 2, Ireland (a division of Penguin Books Ltd).
Penguin Group (Australia), 250 Camberwell Road, Camberwell, Victoria 3124, Australia (a division of
Pearson Australia Group Pty Ltd). Penguin Books India Pvt Ltd, 11 Community Centre, Panchsheel
Park, New Delhi - 110 017, India. Penguin Group (NZ),
67 Apollo Drive, Rosedale, North Shore 0745, Auckland, New Zealand (a division of Pearson New Zealand
Ltd). Penguin Books (South Africa) (Pty) Ltd, 24 Sturdee Avenue, Rosebank, Johannesburg 2196,
South Africa. Penguin Books Ltd, Registered Offices: 80 Strand, London WC2R 0RL, England.

Design by Semadar Megged. The text is set in 16-point Horley Old Style.
The illustrations are rendered in pen-and-ink and watercolors.

Library of Congress Cataloging-in-Publication Data
Gorbachev, Valeri.
Christopher counting / Valeri Gorbachev. p. cm.
Summary: When Christopher Rabbit learns to count in school, he enjoys it so much
that he counts everything in sight, including how many baskets his friends make
when they play basketball and how many peas and carrots are on his plate.
[1. Counting—Fiction. 2. Rabbits—Fiction. 3. Animals—Fiction.] I. Title.
PZ7.G6475Chr 2008 [E]—dc22 2007023642
ISBN 978-0-399-24629-6
10 9 8 7 6 5 4 3 2 1

Valeri Gorbachev

Christopher Counting

Philomel Books

C hildren, today we are going to learn how to count," said
Ms. Goat. She held up ten oranges, one at a time.

"Repeat after me: one, two, three, four, five, six, seven, eight,
nine, ten."

"One, two, three, four, five, six, seven, eight, nine, ten,"
repeated all the children in the class.

All day long the class counted.

Christopher Rabbit loved the idea of counting.
"I can count everything," he said after school was over.

"One, two, three, four," he practiced as he walked home.

"We learned how to count today," Christopher said to Mother Rabbit when she greeted him at the door.

"Look: one, two notebooks, two, three pencils, four, five, six crayons."

He counted everything in his backpack.

Then Christopher counted the fish in his aquarium,
and the toys in the toy box.

The plates and cups in the kitchen,
and the boots, shoes, and sneakers in the hallway.

When he finished counting
everything in the house, Christopher
went outside.

"One, two, three," he counted as
he walked down the steps.

There were so many flowers in the meadow, he only
counted the petals on one.

When Beaver saw Christopher counting lilies at the pond, he said, "Come on, skip stones with me."

"No, thanks," said Christopher. "I'm too busy counting. I'd rather count how many times your stone will skip on the water.

"I love counting," he said to Beaver as he went on.

He counted the butterflies in the air,
and the ants on the ground.

Until he heard Little Chipmunk call out, "Hey, Christopher! We are going to play basketball with the Herons. Come play with us!"

"No, thanks," said Christopher. "Not today. I'd rather count
how many baskets you make. One . . . two . . . three . . ."
"You count very well," said a Heron.
"I love counting," said Christopher.

Then he left to find something else to count when he came
upon Mole. He was counting as well.

"Hey, Mole," said Christopher. "Are you practicing
counting, too?"

"No," said Mole. "I am playing hide-and-seek with my friends. Come play with us, Christopher."

"Yes," Christopher said. "I would love to play."

Christopher shut his eyes and counted to himself:
"One, two, three, four, five, six, seven, eight, nine, ten . . ."
He was getting very good!

Then Christopher went to find all his friends.

"One," he counted out loud as he found Turtle hiding in his shell.

"Two," he counted when he saw Fox next to the log.

"Three," he counted as he found Skunk behind the tree.
"Four," he counted when he found Mole hiding in a hill.

"Five," counted Christopher as he found the Mice under the tree trunk.

"Oops," he said. "My mistake! It's five, six, seven, eight, nine!"

And so all the friends played hide-and-seek until the sun hid behind the trees. Then Christopher went home.

Christopher tried to count as he ate his supper. The peas on his plate. The carrots in his soup.

After supper, he sat in the big chair and yawned and yawned.

"I am very sleepy," he said. "I have already yawned seven times."

"It's bedtime," said Mother Rabbit. "Honey, put on your pajamas and go to bed."

"Wait," said Christopher. "I forgot to count something!"

He went out to the porch and stared at the night sky. "One, two, three . . . oh no!" cried Christopher. "It's impossible! There are just too many stars to count."